SP

To my sweet Loukoumi and our amazing Dean.

LOUKOUMI

Nick Katsoris
Illustrated by: P S Babu

Deep in the mountains of Greece was a little lamb named Loukoumi. Greece was where Loukoumi's grandparents were born and Loukoumi spent her summer days there with her family.

Together they played in the fields.

They walked in the mountains.

And they ate olives
under the olive trees.

At the end of one summer,
it was time for Loukoumi
and her family to return to America.
They went to the airport,
but Loukoumi wandered off
and walked onto the
first plane she saw.

The plane took Loukoumi to France.
After it landed she walked off
in search of her mother.
Loukoumi walked all the way
to the Eiffel tower, but her
mother was nowhere to be found.
Loukoumi started to cry.
Then all of a sudden a cat named Fistiki
came up behind her.
"What's the matter?" Fistiki asked.
"I lost my family," Loukoumi said,
 sniffling back the tears. "We were supposed
to go home to America, but I got on the
wrong plane and now I am lost.
I am never going to wander off alone again."

Fistiki wanted to help his new friend.
So he walked Loukoumi to the train station
where they boarded a train hoping to
find the way to America.
When the train stopped, Loukoumi
and Fistiki were in Italy.

They walked out of the
train station, and they
walked and walked and walked
until they came to the
Leaning Tower of Pisa.
All of a sudden a dog
named Dean passed by.
"Can I help you?" said Dean.
"I lost my family," Loukoumi said,
sniffling back the tears. "We were supposed
to go to America, but I got on the wrong
plane and then I got on the wrong train
and now I am lost. I am never going
to wander off alone again."

Dean wanted to help his new friends.
"I have a boat in Venice," he said.
"I will help you get home to your family."
And so Dean and Fistiki and Loukoumi
went to the dock and took a ride in
Dean's boat.

They sailed for days with no land in sight.
Finally, they landed in Morocco.
Loukoumi, Fistiki and Dean got off
the boat and walked into the middle
of a vast forest.
Then, all of a sudden a monkey named
Marika swung down from a tree.
"Can I help you with something?"
Marika asked.
"I lost my family," Loukoumi said,
sniffling back the tears.
"We were supposed to
go to America, but I got on the wrong plane,
and then the wrong train and
now the wrong boat.
I am lost! I am never going
to wander off alone again."

Marika felt sorry for the trio and
helped them get to the Moroccan airport.
When they arrived at the airport,
Marika asked for directions and
they boarded a plane headed for America.
The plane landed in New York.
As Loukoumi and Fistiki and Dean and Marika
walked off the plane,
Gus the security guard saw the four friends
walking by themselves.

Gus walked up to Loukoumi and noticed
a tag around her neck with her home address on it.
An hour later Gus brought Loukoumi
and her friends home.

Loukoumi's mother was in the backyard.
She was very sad and wondered if she
was ever going to see Loukoumi again.
As Loukoumi entered the yard,
she ran towards her mother.
Her mother was so happy to see Loukoumi
and to meet Loukoumi's new friends.

Loukoumi breathed a sigh of relief.
"I was supposed to go to America with my family,"
Loukoumi said, "but I got on the wrong plane
and then the wrong train and then the wrong boat,
but my friends helped me get home
and now I am not lost anymore.
I am never going to wander off alone again."

THE
END

Visit Loukoumi at: www.Loukoumi.com